W9-ATB-982

The big race was about to start,
and many cars were taking part.
Red Rover, Grappler, and Sunny Sid
lined up on the starting grid.

ST

Red Rover, with a smiling face
said, "Good luck in this important race."
Grappler replied with a sly grin,
"The same to you, but I will win!"

Then Sunny Sid joined in too,
"I think I'll beat the both of you.
I must admit, I'm very quick,
my yellow colour does the trick."

The starter fired the shot to "GO!"
The cars were off, and they weren't slow.
They rallied hard to take the lead,
showing their amazing speed.

No cars yet tried a silly stunt,
Sunny Sid was near the front.
Red Rover sat close by his side,
while Grappler was not far behind.

The lead kept changing, lap by lap.
As they sped by the crowd would clap.
The cars were many types and colours,
reds, blues, greens, purples, and yellows.

Red Rover fell back in the pack
but Grappler made a quick attack.
He was just about to reach the lead
when a green car flashed past at great speed.

"Oh no!" said Sunny Sid, "He's going to win!"
But Grappler said, "We'll soon catch him.
He thinks he's fast and we are slow,
but there is still so far to go."

Grappler made a sudden dash,
but things can happen in a flash.
All the crowd gasped in suspense
as the purple car sideswiped the fence.

"Just my luck, I've blown a tire."
Grappler's rear wheel had caught on fire.
Sunny Sid laughed as he passed,
and Grappler dropped right back to last.

Into the pit-stop, Grappler turned.
They quickly changed the tire that burned.
"Please hurry up!" he asked the men,
but he barely had to count to ten.

Before he knew it he was out,
he'd catch the rest, he had no doubt,
providing he blew no more tires,
To win this race was his desire.

Then he raced back onto the track
shouting, "OK everyone, I'm back!"
More and more cars Grappler passed,
no longer was he running last.

Accidents were happening too,
a pink car hit hard by a blue.
It overturned, flew in the air,
but the blue car didn't even care.

Red Rover who had been behind
had an idea in his mind.
He'd take a shortcut instead
and use a springboard to jump ahead.

Into the air the red car flew,
where he'd land nobody knew.
He said, "I'll hit the front, or bust,
I hope I don't land deep in dust."

Red Rover landed with a thud,
Buried deep in dirt and mud.
He said, "Well, that idea didn't work.
It's lucky that I am not hurt."

"Bad idea, but worth a try,"
laughed Sunny Sid as he raced by.
Then Grappler passed him, with a smirk,
"I like your new paint colour - dirt."

Two monster trucks came to his aid.
They pushed and pulled with ropes and chains.
Finally they got him free,
he was as nice as he could be.

"I cannot sit around and chat,
I have a lot of cars to catch.
Thank you for the help my friends,
now I have a race to win."

STOP

CLOSED

Red Rover was in a bad mood,
his racing manners very rude.
He slammed hard into Sunny Sid,
and off the track the yellow car slid.

Sunny Sid's eyes opened wide,
Red rover took him by surprise.
"Take that you yellow piece of tin,
this big race is mine to win!"

Sunny Sid said, with a frown,
"Red Rover you are quite a clown!
If I get back up on the track
I'll make sure that I pay you back!"

A crane truck lifted Sunny Sid
who'd toppled over on his lid,
and put him back up on the track,
saying, "In the race you'll soon be back."

In Sunny Sid and Red Rover's wake
Grappler tried to jump the lake.
He sped up fast but jumped too late,
the cold blue water was his fate.

"Oh no!" he said, "This isn't fun.
A wet car engine may not run.
I hope someone can pull me out.
Help me please!" he had to shout.

To his surprise cars tossed in ropes,
this raised his spirits and his hopes.
Sunny Sid, Green car, and Blue,
he'd made new friends, this proved it too.

"We helped you because we thought you'd win,
besides that, purple cars can't swim."
They pulled him out and dried him out
He peeped his horn and gave a shout.

All the cars rejoined the race
and caught up at a rapid pace.
Red rover had been far ahead,
but Grappler suddenly took the lead.

The winners parked upon the podium
At the race inauguration.
As the trophies were awarded
Grappler spoke and was applauded.

"I'd like to thank the other cars,
I'm sure they'll all be future stars.
Thanks officials and the pit-crews,
we couldn't race if not for you."